The Little Band

ALSO BY JAMES SAGE
Illustrated by Warwick Hutton

TO SLEEP

ALSO BY KEIKO NARAHASHI
Written by Mary Serfozo

WHO SAID RED?
WHO WANTS ONE?
RAIN TALK

WRITTEN AND ILLUSTRATED
BY KEIKO NARAHASHI

I HAVE A FRIEND

The Little Band

James Sage
Illustrated by Keiko Narahashi

MARGARET K. MCELDERRY BOOKS
NEW YORK

Collier Macmillan Canada
TORONTO

Maxwell Macmillan International Publishing Group
NEW YORK   OXFORD   SINGAPORE   SYDNEY

For Elizabeth
J. S.

For Micah and Joy
K. N.

Text copyright © 1991 by James Sage
Illustrations copyright © 1991 by Keiko Narahashi

Margaret K. McElderry Books
Macmillan Publishing Company
866 Third Avenue
New York, NY 10022

Collier Macmillan Canada, Inc.
1200 Eglinton Avenue East
Suite 200
Don Mills, Ontario M3C 3N1

First edition
Printed in Hong Kong by South China Printing Company (1988) Ltd.
10 9 8 7 6 5 4 3 2 1

Library of Congress Cataloging-in-Publication Data

Sage, James.
The little band /James Sage ; illustrated by Keiko Narahashi. —
1st ed.
p.   cm.
Summary: A little band marches through town delighting everyone
with its beautiful music.
ISBN 0-689-50516-7
[1. Bands (Music)—Fiction.] I. Narahashi, Keiko, ill.
II. Title.
PZ7.S1304Li 1991 [E]—dc20
90-40089 CIP AC

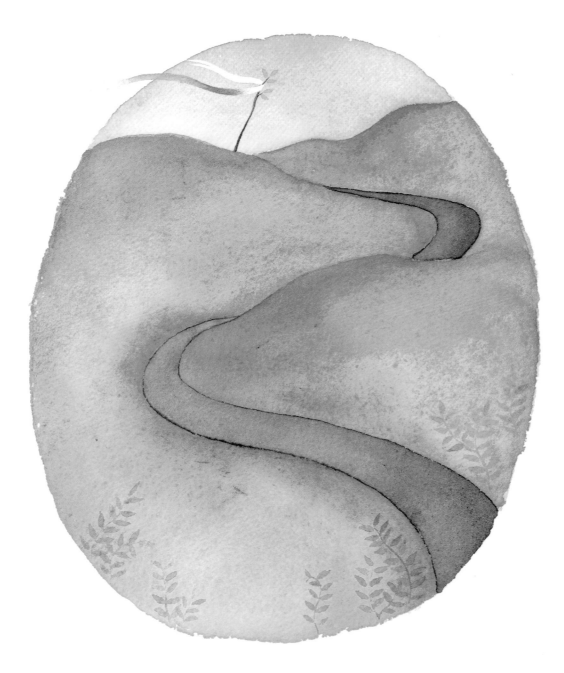

At first there was the sound of faraway music.

Then the little band appeared.
They marched across the bridge and into town.
"Who are they?" wondered the mailman.

"Why are they here?"
asked the shoppers in the market.
"Where are they going?"
demanded the policeman.
But there were no answers.
Without missing a beat,
the little band marched on.

"Wait!" called the mayor,
who wanted to give a speech of welcome.
But the little band did not wait.
They marched past the town officials,
past the workmen enjoying a rest,
past the bride and groom leaving church,
past the smiling faces in the playground.

The music pleased one man so much,
he stood on his head in excitement,

while further down the street,
a woman did a little dance as she hung up her washing.

"Charming! Charming!" murmured the old folks
as they rocked to the rhythm of the drum.

"What a wonder!" exclaimed the sea captain,
who thought he had seen everything.

The music made the dogs bark
and the cats howl
and the chickens cluck
and the sheep baa with contentment.

The farmer and his wife waved a friendly hello.
So did the apple pickers in the orchard,
and the cyclists puffing up the hill,
and the campers pitching their tents
by the side of the lake.

"Amazing!" cried the fishermen,
as fish began to leap around them.

Away, away marched the little band,
through the woods,
across the meadows,

and along the cliffs, high above the sea.
Into the distance they marched,
leaving behind no hint of who they were,
or why they had come, or where they were going.

But long afterward, people remembered
their beautiful faraway music.

And nothing was ever the same again.